Counting Animals with
Lily and Milo

Pauline Oud

Clavis

NEW YORK

Lily and Milo are walking in the meadow.
"I wonder if we will see any animals," Milo says.
Look! There is a big cow.
The cow moos. Mooooo!

1

Lily counts one cow.
One!

2

The cow is not alone. Look at that!
"The cow has calves," Milo cries out. "Do you see?"

How many calves do you count?
One, two.
Two!

3

What animal do Lily and Milo see next?
It's white and wears a warm woolen coat.
"A sheep," Milo calls out. "With little sheep, too."
"Those are lambs," Lily says.

How many little white lambs do you count?
One, two, three.
Three!

"Hey," Milo calls. "What's that?"
"Little birds," Lily says. "They are hungry."
Mommy Bird has a worm in her beak.

Take a close look.
How many little birds do you count?
One, two, three, four.
Four!

4

Meow, meow. The cat mews quietly.
Who is she calling to?
Her little ones are cuddled together in the hay.
"Oh," Lily whispers, "they're so cute!"

Time for a nap.
How many kittens do you count?
One, two, three, four, five.
Five!

5

Lily and Milo visit the chicken coop.
A chicken is resting on a perch.
"Do you think she laid some eggs?" asks Milo.
"Yes," Lily says. "Look over here."
Lily and Milo find eggs in a bed of straw.

How many eggs do you count?
One, two, three, four,
five, six. Six!

6

"Look," Milo calls.
"A mommy duck is swimming
in the water!"
"Yes, with her ducklings,"
Lily says with a smile.
"Milo, did you see?"

Take a look in the pond.
Can you count the ducklings?
One, two, three, four, five, six, seven.
Seven!

7

Hey, what animal
do Lily and Milo see next?
It's pink and lying in the mud.
"A pig!" Milo calls.
"And she's feeding her piglets," says Lily.

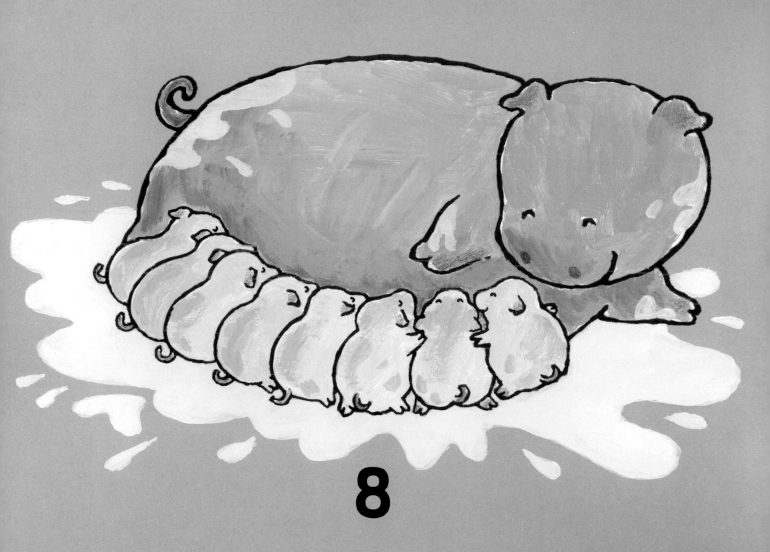

8

How many piglets are having their lunch?
One, two, three, four, five, six, seven, eight.
Eight!

Lily and Milo walk back to the meadow.
"So many beautiful flowers," Lily calls.
"And butterflies!" cries Milo.

So many butterflies, too!
Can you count them with Milo?
One, two, three, four, five, six,
seven, eight, nine.
Nine!

9

Lily and Milo see a fish jump in the pond.
They go closer to take a look.

Busy fish are swimming
in the water.
How many fish do they
count? One, two, three,
four, five, six, seven, eight,
nine, ten.
Ten!

10

Lily and Milo head home.
They counted a lot of animals today.
1 cow, 2 calves, 3 lambs, 4 birds,
5 kittens, 6 eggs, 7 ducklings,
8 piglets, 9 butterflies, and 10 swimming fish.

But, wait a minute . . .
What is that in their cart?
It's white and round and is making a noise.
Crack . . . crack . . .

"A chick!" Milo cries.
"Come," Lily says sweetly.
"We'll take you to your mommy."
One chick. One.

1